A Trip to Canada
100 Tanka by Koichi Kansaku
in 5 Languages

カナダへの旅
神作光一百首歌
〈英・仏・独・中訳付き〉

郡　山　　直 英訳
朝比奈美知子 仏訳
堀　　光　男 独訳
続　　三　義 中訳

*Translated
by*
*Naoshi Koriyama into English,
Michiko Asahina into French,
Mitsuo Hori into German,
Xu Sanyi into Chinese*

朝日出版社

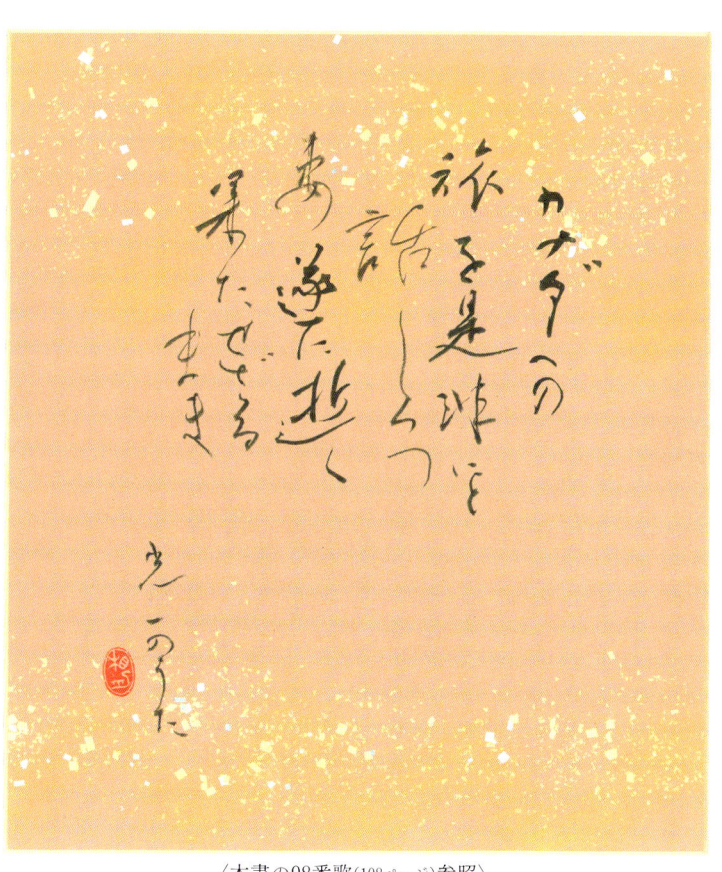

〈本書の98番歌(108ページ)参照〉

カナダへの旅　目次

- 5 ・ まえがき
- 7 ・ Preface
- 9 ・ カナダへの旅
- 111 ・『カナダへの旅　神作光一百首歌』に寄せて　　郡山　直
- 115 ・ A Tribute from a Translator　　*Naoshi Koriyama*

口絵　三宅相舟 書

まえがき

　　　　　　　　　　　　　　歌人　神作光一

　思い返しますと、私が短歌の創作に従事してから、55年ほどの歳月が経過しています。その間、長期にわたって念願していることは、短歌は、声調を重んじ、平明な表現の中に、滋味の感じられるものでありたい。その上、できれば印象の鮮明な作品でありたい、ということであります。しかし、その道は、今なお果てしもなく遠いと思います。

　まさに、「日暮れて道遠し」(『史記』) という感慨が一入(ひとしお)であります。それゆえに、これから後も、こつこつと努力し、より高く、より深い境地を目ざして、一歩一歩と歩み続けてゆくつもりであります。

　なお、本書の刊行のために、ご多忙中のところ、翻訳のお仕事を進めてくださいました郡山直先生（英訳）、堀光男先生（独訳）、朝比奈美知子先生（仏訳）、続三義先生（中訳）という四人の先生方のご芳情に対して、深く感謝の意を捧げたいと考えます。いろいろと有難うございました。

　なお、本書の書名『カナダへの旅』は、次の一首から採りました。

　　○カナダへの旅を是非にと話しつつ
　　　妻遂に逝く果たせざるまま　　　　　（本書98番歌）

因みに、この書名の拠り所となった一首を、書家として著名な三宅相舟先生が色紙にご染筆くださり、本書の巻頭の口絵として飾ることをご高配くださいました。そのお心づかいに対し、ここで心からなる感謝の意を捧げる次第です。

　ここで日本の和歌史における「百首歌」のことについて、簡潔にコメントしておきたいと思います。現在から見て、およそ1000年ほど前、男性歌人では曾祢好忠（そねのよしただ）の『好忠百首』、源順（みなもとのしたごう）の『順百首』、僧侶歌人でもあった恵慶（えぎょう）の『恵慶百首』などが知られています。一方、女流歌人では、相模（さがみ）の『相模百首』が名高いと言えます。いずれも平安中期の「百首歌」歌人として、今なお広く愛読され続けています。そうした「百首歌」の流れの末尾に、本書が加わることになれば、著者としての私の喜びは、まことに大きいと言えます。

　なお、本書の出版をご快諾くださいました朝日出版社およびご担当の清水浩一様のご芳情に対しても深い感謝の意を捧げたいと思います。

2011年9月20日

Preface

When I look back, I realize that some 55 years has passed since I began to write tanka. During that long period of time I have always wished my tanka to have a good tone of voice and a plain, simple expression, in which the reader could feel a deep delicacy. Moreover, I have wished it to give a vivid impression, if possible. My goal, however, seems a long way off.

I certainly feel, "Night is falling, but there is a long way to go," just as written in the Chinese classic, *Shih-chi*, (Historical Records). Therefore, I make up my mind to make constant efforts even from now on, aiming at a higher and deeper field of tanka, taking one steady step after another.

I am deeply grateful to all the translators who were kind enough to work to produce this book, Mr. Naoshi Koriyama translating these tanka into English, Mr. Mitsuo Hori into German, Ms. Michiko Asahina into French, and Mr. Xu Sanyi into Chinese. I can't express my deep gratitude to them in words.

The title of this book is taken from the following tanka. (No. 98).

> *My wife and I planned, saying*
> *we would take a trip*
> *to Canada by any means,*
> *but she is gone*
> *without realizing the plan.*

And Mr. Soshu Miyake, a noted calligrapher, was kind enough to write with a brush on a special card the tanka from which the title of this book is taken, and I was able to grace this book with his calligraphy as a frontispiece. For his kindness I'd like to express my hearty gratitude.

Incidentally, I would like to briefly refer to a few collections of "100 Tanka" in the history of Japanese tanka. About 1000 years ago, male tanka poets made their collections of "100 Tanka" : Soneno Yoshitada making "Yoshitada's 100 Tanka"; Minamotono Shitago "Shitago's 100 Tanka"; and Egyo, a monk poet, "Egyo's 100 Tanka." They are well-known, while a female tanka poet, Sagami, made her collection, "Sagami's 100 Tanka" which is also famous. They are all well-known as "100 tanka poets" and still widely read and loved by people today. I would be more than happy, if this book could follow in their footsteps.

And I am grateful to Mr. Koichi Shimizu of Asahi Press for accepting my request to have this book published.

September 20, 2011

Koichi Kansaku
Translated by Naoshi Koriyama

カナダへの
旅を是非にと
話しつつ
妻遂に逝く
果たせざるまま

Kanada heno
Tabiwo zehinito
Hanashitsutsu
Tsuma tsuini yuku
Hatasezarumama

1. 帰り行ける君は家へと着く頃か
　　霙降る夜のスタンドを消す
　　　(みぞれ)

Leaving me here,
you may have got home
by now.
I turn off my desk lamp.
It's sleeting out.

Pensant à toi,
Qui, étant partie de chez moi,
Serais maintenant à la maison,
J'éteins ma lampe.
Une nuit sous la neige fondue.

Draußen gibt's Schneeregen.
Ist es die Zeit, wo Du gerade nach Hause kommst,
nachdem Du mich verlassen hast?
Ich mache das Licht der Tischlampe aus.

雨夹雪之夜，
君*回自家去，　　　　　　*作者未婚妻。
估摸已到家，
才把台灯熄。

2. 共に歩むただそれだけで事足れり
　　大磯の海まぶしく光る

Just walking together
side by side
is gratifying.
The sea of Oiso shines
brightly.

Je ne demanderais rien
Que de marcher ensemble
Avec toi, bien-aimée,
En regardant la mer d'Ôiso
En pleine lumière.

Es ist schon genug,
wenn wir zusammen gehen
auf dem Strand von Oiso.
Das Meer leuchtet blendend.

两人并肩走，
仅此足满意，
大矶海浩瀚，
碧波晃眼晕。

3. 野はなべて新しき色に光りたり
　　支へゆかんと手を組み合はす

All the fields shine
in a new light.
I place my hands together,
vowing,
"I will support her with all my might."

En regardant
Les champs devant nous,
Tout lumineux en ses couleurs fraîches,
Restons les mains dans les mains,
Pour éterniser nos liens.

Auf dem Feld leuchtet
alles mit neuen Farben.
Da wir uns stutzen wollen,
haken wir uns miteinander ein.

原野阳光映新绿，
手挽手，
共约定：
相互扶持朝前行！

4.　「若き師」と七百の女高生に迎へられ
　　　歩き方まで噂されゐる

"The young teacher"
is welcomed
by 700 high schoolgirls.
They are already chatting
about my way of walking.

Me voilà, jeune professeur,
Devant sept cents jeunes filles,
Tellement intéressées à mon égard :
Elles parlent déjà
De ma manière de marcher.

Als „junger Lehrer"
bin ich von 700 Schülerinnen empfangen,
und sie quatschen schon darüber,
wie die Art meines Gangs ist.

七百女高生,
迎我进讲堂,
"这位老师真年轻！"
"走路姿势是那样！"

5.　やはらかく蓮は煮えしやと母は問ふ
　　自炊生活の我に文(ふみ)して

"Did you cook
the lotus roots till they got tender?"
my mother asks me in her letter,
when I started cooking
my own meals.

La cuisson de la racine de lotus ?
Une petite question
Dans la lettre
Où ma mère se soucie de moi,
Moi, qui fais ma cuisine moi-même.

Meine Mutter hat mir einen Brief
geschrieben und fragt mich,
der ich selbst koche,
ob ich Lotos weich gekocht habe.

一个人生活，
饮食自动手，
老母来信问：
"莲藕煮软否？"

6. 鉄骨を組む閃光が冴ゆるなり
　　たそがれ迫るビルの屋上

As they put up
iron frames,
sparks flash
atop a building under construction
at evening twilight.

Des étincelles vives
Au crépuscule
Jaillissant de charpentes de fer
Qu'on essaie de dresser,
Observées du haut de l'mmeuble.

In der Abenddämmerung
ist es das Blitzlicht
des Stahlgerüstes klar zu sehen
auf dem Flachdach eines Hochhauses.

黄昏将近楼顶站，
钢架焊接闪光寒。

7.　冷え著(しる)き鉄筋校舎の一室に
　　　一つの考証もてあましゐる

In a very cold room
of a concrete school building
I'm not feeling competent enough
to solve a problem,
while examining its background.

Tout seul dans une salle
De l'immeuble en béton,
Glacé jusqu'aux os,
Je ne termine jamais cette étude
Qui me préoccupe toujours.

In einem sehr kalten Klassenzimmer
der von Stahlgerüst gebauten Schüle
weiss ich nichit, was ich mit der Erforschung
historischer Quellen anfangen soll.

钢筋校舍寒气逼,
独处一室苦考据,
仍是无结论。

8. 　菊開く季節(とき)となりたり少しづつ
　　　君を迎へる日が近づきぬ

The season
of chrysanthemums is
drawing near little by little.
The day of welcoming you
is approaching.

Dans cette saison
Fleurissante de chrysanthèmes.
S'approche le jour,
Où toi, bien aimée,
Tu seras parmi les nôtres.

Es ist die Blütezeit der Chrysanthemen gekommen.
Es nähert sich auch die Zeit,
wo ich Dich allmählich
empfangen werde.

已是菊花盛开季,
迎君之日渐临莅。

9.　共に来て涼しげなる色選びをり
　　　二人の部屋につけるカーテン

We have come
together,
to choose curtains
of a cool color
for our room.

Sortant ensemble,
Nous avons choisi,
Toi et moi,
Un rideau d'une couleur fraîche,
Qui ornera bientôt notre chambre.

Sie kommen zu zweit
und wählen kühle Farben
des Vorhangs
für ihr Zimmer.

两人一起来,
挑选凉爽色,
房间两人住,
窗帘不可缺。

10.　研一が玩具(おもちゃ)のバット手に遊ぶ
　　　思はぬ場所へボール飛ばして

Kenichi* is playing　　　　　　*The author's son
with his toy bat,
hitting a ball
to a place
quite unexpected.

Mon filis Kenichi s'amuse,
Bâton de baseball à la main,
À envoyer la balle
Dans des directions
Les plus fantaisistes.

Ken-itchi spielt
mit einem (Baseball-)Stock
und der Ball fliegt weg
nach einem unerwarteten Ort.

玩具棒球棒，
研一*把手玩，　　　　　　*作者之长子。
棒球飞哪里，
只有天晓知。

11.　這ひて坐りつかまり立ちしてまた坐り
　　　典子やうやく次の間へ行く

Our daughter, Noriko,
crawls, and sits up,
and stands holding onto something,
then sits down again,
and now manages to move into a next room.

Elle avance, en se traînant,
Un instant de repos, assise,
Debout, assise encore une fois — et
Voilà enfin qu'elle arrive,
Noriko, à la pièce annexe.

Meine Tochter Noriko
kriecht, sitzt, steht
und wieder sitzt,
geht schließlich ins nächsten Zimmer.

爬爬坐,
扶物站,
又坐下。
隔壁房间里,
典子*终抵达。　　　　　　　*作者之长女。

12. 車降り檜扇(ひあふぎ)の花教へ給ふ
　　　師に従(つ)きて来し秋の信濃路

I get off the car
on my trip to Shinano in autumn,
following my mentor.
He shows me
blackberry lilies.

Suivant mon maître,
Qui, à la sortie de la voiture,
Me désigne les fleurs d'iris tigré,
Me voilà dans le chemin
De Shinano en automne.

Auf dem Herbstweg von Shinano
folge ich meinem Lehrer,
der vom Auto.aussteigt und zeigt
die Blumen von Hiaogi.

深秋信浓路*,　　　　　　　　　*旧国名，今日本长野县。
随师**一同来，　　　　　　　　**作者之恩师平野宣纪。
下车师教诲：
"此乃黑莓花。"

13. 　白に佇ち緋に佇ちシャッター切りてをり
　　　牡丹満開の寺暮るるまで

Now stopping by white peonies,
now stopping by scarlet ones,
I keep clicking the shutter,
until night falls on the temple,
where peonies are in full bloom.

Coups d'appareils de photo
Devant celles qui sont blanches,
Devant celles pourpres,
Au temple de pivoines en pleine floraison,
Jusqu'au crépuscule du soir.

Im Tempelbezirk sind Päonien in voller Blüte.
Ich stehe mal vor weiße, mal vor rote Päonien,
und drücke auf den Auslöser,
bis es am Abend dunkel wird,

逢白止步看，
遇绯亦停观，
快门摁不止，
直到牡丹盛开寺暮时。

14.　逃げられたる小鳥のことを電話にて
　　　知らせ来る典子の潤[うる]みたる声

As she tells me on the phone
about the bird that flew away
from the cage,
Noriko's voice sounds moist
with tears.

Avec une voix
Humide de larme
Noriko me parle au téléphone
De son petit oiseau
Qui s'est enfui.

Mit tauriger Stimme läßt Noriko (meine Tochter)
mich telephonisch wissen,
dass ihr Vöglein
weggeflogen ist.

"小鸟逃走啦！"
典子电话告我知,
声音润润湿。

15.　事切れたる母の背中を拭ひつつ
　　　　床擦れの傷に息を飲みをり

Wiping the back
of my deceased mother
bruised with bedsores,
I keep holding
my breath.

Essuyant le dos de ma mère
Qui a rendu son âme,
J'ai le souffle coupé :
Des escarres dans ses reins,
Signes de son alitement chronique.

Wärend ich meiner gestorbenen Mutter
den Rücken wische (wasche),
entdeckte ich die Wunde
und halte ich den Atem an.

慈母终闭目，
为母拭背脊，
褥疮伤累累，
惊叹倒吸气。

16.　　自動車のカーブするたび膝上に
　　　　抱(かか)へし母の骨壺の鳴る

At each turn of the car
along the winding road,
my mother's urn
on my lap
rustles.

Chaque virement de la voiture funèbre,
Fait claquer légèrement
Les cendres de ma mère,
Contenues dans le pot
Que je tiens sur les genoux.

Immer wenn unser Wagen eine Kurve macht,
tönt der Kasten der Gebeine
von meiner Mutter, den ich mir
auf dem Schoß halte.

汽车每拐弯，
膝上慈母骨灰盒，
声响总不断。

17.　　傘の上に桜の花びら付きゐたり
　　　　ホームにて傘を畳みゆくとき

When I fold
my folding umbrella
on the platform,
I see some cherry blossom petals
sticking to the umbrella.

Sensation du printemps
Sur le quai de la gare,
Quand je trouve quelques pétales
De cerisiers fleurissants
Collés sur mon parapluie que je replie.

Als ich auf dem Bahnhof laufend
meinen Regenschirm zusammenhielt,
fand ich Blütenblaetter des Kirschbaums.
auf dem Schirm steckend.

进入火车站,
伫立月台边,
收起折叠伞,
上有樱花瓣。

18.　せり既に済みて木箱は乾きゆく
　　　昼の市場(いちば)に匂ひ鋭く

At the fish market*　　　　　*The fish market in Tsukiji,
the auction sale is　　　　　　Tokyo
now over.
Wooden boxes get dry,
while the smell is pungent at the market at noon.

Finie la vente à la criée,
Les caisses en bois
Commencent déjà à sécher
Dans les halles
Pleines encore d'odeurs intenses.

Auktionsmarkt ist schon zu Ende
und Holzkisten werden trocken.
Aber auf dem Marktplatz am Mittag
riecht es noch stark nach Fisch.

拍卖已结束，
木箱渐次干，
正午鱼市场*，　　　　　　　*日本东京筑地之海鲜批发市场，
鱼腥冲鼻孔。　　　　　　　　以凌晨海鲜拍卖市场闻名。

19. 里芋の葉を翻す風ありて
　　　ローカル線の駅に降り立つ

<small>ひるがへ</small>

Winds turn over
the leaves of taros,
when I get off the train
at a station
on a local railway line.

Par un vent frais
Qui souffle sur les colocases,
En renversant leurs feuilles,
Je descends à une station
Du chemin de fer local.

Der Wind weht die Blaetter
von Taro-Kartoffeln.
Ich steige auf den Bahnhof
einer Lokallinie aus.

地方线，
小车站，
我下车，
月台站，
微风吹得芋叶转。

20.　ベレー帽飛ばすばかりに吹きつける
　　　湖(みづうみ)からの湿り持つ風

My beret cap
is almost blown away
by the moist winds
blowing
from the lake.

L'assaut violent
D'un vent humide
Venant du lac
Comme pour emporter loin
Mon béret.

Der feuchte Wind vom See
bläst mich ins Gesicht,
Der Wind wollte mir
die Baskenmütze fliegen lassen.

湖上来风湿且潮，
几乎吹掉鸭舌帽。

21.　切り立てる岩壁登る人遠し
　　　かすかに動く気配見せつつ

Someone is climbing
up the precipitous cliff
in the distance, showing
a sign
of slight moving.

Là-bas, des gens
Gravissant le rocher escarpé !
Leurs mouvements
Sont bien subtiles,
Vus de loin !

Jemand erklettert
eine steile Felsenwand
weit in der Ferne, indem er
eine schwache Bewegung zeigt.

陡峭绝壁岩,
有人在登攀,
远处看,
只见蠕蠕动动一点点。

22. 僅かなる窪みにも雨はたまれるか
　　車次々はねあげて過ぐ

Rainwater must have
collected even in shallow hollows
on the street.
One car after another passes,
splashing.

Sur de petites flaques d'eau
Que la pluie fait apparaître,
Des véhicules passent
Un à un, en hâte,
Faisant rejaillir de l'eau.

Regenwasser könnte sich sammeln
eben in einer kleinen Vertiefung der Strasse.
Ein Wagen nach dem andern
läuft aufsplitzend vorbei.

路上小洼处，
或可积点雨，
车辆频繁过，
雨水尽溅起。

23.　帰り来てコートも脱がぬに数本の
　　　　電話次々かかり来る夜

Even before I take off
my coat on coming home,
several phone calls come,
one after another,
at night.

Arrivé à la maison,
Avant même d'enlever le manteau,
Me voilà sous l'assaut
De plusieurs appels téléphoniques
Qui s'ensuivent.

Wenn ich des abends nach Hause komme,
klingelt das Telefon mehrmals
eines nach dem andern,
eben bevor ich meinen Mantel abziehe.

归来尚未脱外套，
几个电话不停叫，
是今宵。

24.　　紫に咲ける菖蒲の一ところ
　　　　花明かりして墓地へと続く

A spot
where a cluster of purple irises are in bloom
is brightened by the flowers.
The space leads
to a cemetery.

Sur l'étendue violette
Des champs de fleurs d'iris,
Se découpe une route,
Étrangement éclairée,
Qui conduit au cimetière.

Ein Teil von violetten Wasserlilie
ist in voller Blüte,
und der Ort führt mich
zu einem Friedhof.

一丛菖蒲开，
紫花亮且鲜，
花明耀周边，
直通到陵园。

25.　鼓笛隊の一員としてパレードする
　　　娘思ひつつ編集続く

I keep doing
my editorial work,
thinking of my daughter
who will parade
in the drum and fife band.

Je suis toujours occupé
Par le travail rédactionnel,
En me figurant ma fille,
Marchant en parade
Parmi les musiciens du défilé.

Wärend ich meine Arbeit der Redaktion fortsetze,
denke ich an meine Tochter,
die als ein Mitglied von Trommler und Pfeifer
eine Parade abhielt.

鼓笛乐方阵,
娇女在其中。
遥想女舞姿,
编辑手不停。

26.　文化祭の雑踏を少し離れたる
　　　所に竹刀(しなひ)打ち合ふ音す

At some distance
away from hustle and bustle
of school festival,
I hear sounds
of bamboo swords* exchanging blows.
　　　　　　　　　　*Used in Japanese fencing

Un peu à l'écart de la foule,
Visitant la fête culturelle de l'école,
On entend quelque part
Des claquements limpides
De sabres de bambou.

Am Ort ein bischen entfernt
vom Gedrange des Tages der offenen Türen
in der Schule höre ich Klänge
der fechtenden Bambusschwerte.

文化节*,
声喧闹。
稍稍离开处,
竹刀**交劈声楚楚。

*日本高中、大学在11月初举行的文化活动。

**日本"剑道"所用器械。

27.　野の中の道光りつつ行く車
　　　　下(くだ)りのリフトに見え隠れする

As I look down
from the descending lift,
I see cars going along the road through fields
shining in the sun,
now appearing, now disappearing.

Du télésiège en descente
J'entrevois par moments
Des voitures qui passent,
Lumineuses, brillantes,
À travers les champs de verdure.

Als ich vom hinunterfahrenden Lift aus
unterschaue, sehe ich fahrende Wagen
auf dem Felderweg, im Sonnenschein
mal sichtbar, mal unsichtbar werdend.

原野道路上，
车行光闪闪，
下行缆车中观看，
时隐又时现。

28.　健やかに傘寿となれる師の御声
　　　凛として歌の道説き給ふ

My old mentor
is now 80 years old
in good health.
He gives a lecture about tanka
in a crisp voice.

Ayant quatre-vingts ans
Dans sa parfaite santé
Mon maître me montre,
Avec cette voix déterminée,
Le chemin de l'art poétique.

Mein alter Lehrer, der jetzt 80 Jahre alt ist,
ist immer noch gesund,
und er hält uns eine Vorlesung über Tanka
in proper Stimme.

吾师*身矍铄，
伞寿**八十整，
力说歌之道，
声音亮且洪。

*作者之恩师平野宣纪。

**日文"伞"字简写为八字下面一个十字，"伞寿"即"八十大寿"。

29. 背を丸め日記を綴りゐる父よ
　　　　寂しくあらん母亡き五年(ごねん)

In a stooping position,
Father is writing his diary.
He must be lonely.
It's been five years
since Mother passed away.

Mon père qui écrit son journal,
Dos courbé,
Comment n'aurait-il pas la solitude
Depuis cinq ans,
Depuis la mort de ma mère.

Mein Vater macht einen Katzenbuckel
und führt sein Tagebuch.
Sicher fühlt er sich allein,
da meine Mutter vor 5 Jahren gestorben ist.

父亲记日记，
背脊已躬屈，
母逝五载过，
安能不寂寞？

30. 案内して葛飾真間を巡りゆく
　　秋蜻蛉飛ぶ午後のひととき

I conduct a group,
taking them around Katsushika-Mama
in the afternoon
when dragon flies of autumn
are flying.

Guide d'une promenade ambulante
À travers les champs de Katsushika-mama
Je savoure un moment d'automne ;
L'après-midi,
Où passent des libellules.

Eines Nachmittags führe eine Gruppe
und mache einen Rundgang
in Katsushika-Mama,
wo Herbst-Libellen fliegen.

我带学生游，
葛饰真间巡，
午后一时刻，
秋蜻蜓舞飞。

*葛饰，旧郡名，今日本东京都葛饰区及千叶县市川市一带。真间，今千叶县市川市，以"真间手儿奈"闻名。

31.　川明かり幽(かそ)けく及ぶ位置を占め
　　　白秋(はくしう)旧居はひそとして建つ

The gleam on the river's surface
faintly reaches the place,
where Hakushu's* old house
stands
quietly.

*Kitahara Hakushu, a poet (1885–1942)

Sur l'endroit
Éclairé subtilement
Par la lueur vague de la rivière,
Se dresse silencieux
L'ancienne demeure de Hakushû.

Das alte Haus von Hakushu steht still,
und nimmt eine Position ein,
wo der Schimmer des Flusses
heimlich erreicht.

小河水光亮，
微光照河堤，
就在河水光照处，
白秋*旧居立。

*北原白秋（1885-1942），日本著名短歌诗人。

32.　書展見る約束をして妻の待つ
　　　デパートに向かふ午後のひと時

At an afternoon hour
I walk
toward the department store
where my wife and I promised to meet
before going to see a calligraphy exhibit.

Un après-midi
Qui me presse vers le grand magasin.
C'est le rendez-vous
Fixé avec ma femme
Pour une exposition de calligraphie.

An einem Nachmittag
gehe ich nach dem Kaufhaus,
wo meine Frau auf mich wartet,
um zusammen eine Kalligraphie-Ausstellung zu sehen.

相约去看书法展,
妻子等在百货店,
我正去相见,
午后一时间。

33. 北白川 衣川越え西行の
　　詠める束稲の山遠く見ゆ

Going across the Kitashira River
and the Koromo River,
I see Mt. Tabashine*
far in the distance,
which Saigyo** sang of.

*A mountain in Iwate Prefecture, famous for cherry blossoms

**A priest-poet (1118–1190)

À Kitashirakawa,
Traversant la rivière Koromo,
J'ai vu au loin
Le mont Tabashine,
Admiré jadis par Saigyô.

Über den Kitashirakawa-Fluss
und den Koromogawa-Fluss
sehe ich ferne den Tabashine-Berg,
von dem Saigyo gedichtet hat.

跨过北白川*,
再渡过衣川*,
西行**曾咏束稻山***,
远处可望见。

*均为日本岩手县内河流。
**日本平安时代歌僧（1118-1190）。
***日本岩手县内山峰，以樱花著称。

34. 初春の日が神域に及びゐて
　　　神官の履く浅沓光る

The sun
of early spring shines
over the shrine's precincts,
and the Shinto priest's clogs
gleam.

L'aurore du matin
Du jour de l'an
Remplit le sanctuaire shintoïste,
Faisant scintiller
Les chaussures plates du prêtre.

Die Sonne des Frühlings
scheint über den Tempelbezik,
und lichtet die seichten Schuhe
des Priesters.

初春第一天，
阳光照神域，
神官履浅沓*，
烨烨闪光华。

*日本神社中神官所穿桐木制浅木屐。

35. 小手毬と雪柳との弁別を
　　　言ひつつ妻は花を活けゆく

My wife arranges
flowers
in a vase,
mentioning the difference
between the Reeves spirea and the Thunberg spirea.

Ma femme met artistiquement
Les fleurs dans le vase,
En me disant la difference
Entre la spirée hypercifolia
Et la spirée thunbergii.

Meine Frau stellt Blumen in eine Vase,
indem sie erklärt den Unterschied
zwischen Spierstrauch
und Kantonspierstrauch.

这是麻叶绣线菊,
这是珍珠花,
妻子边说俩不同,
边把花儿插。

36. 頭注に未詳とありし語の考証
　　　漸くなし得て明け方となる

By the time
I have managed to discover
the historical background
of a word specified as "unknown" in the headnote,
the day begins to break.

Les premières lueurs du jour m'entoure ;
Moi, qui viens d'achever
Une recherche exhaustive
Pour un mot hermétique
Dont les sources étaient inconnues.

In der Zeit, als ich historische Quelle
vom Wort bezeichnet mit „Unbekannt",
erforscht habe,
ist der Tag schon angebrochen.

书页有眉批，
"此语意未详。"
考据终有果，
东方现曙光。

37.　　日々使ふ白墨(チョーク)の僅かな湿(しめ)りにて
　　　　梅雨(つゆ)近しと知る教師の吾は

By feeling the slight moisture
of the chalk
I use every day,
I, being a teacher, can tell
the rainy season approaching.

À cette humidité légère
Du morceau de craie
Que j'utilise tous les jours,
Je sens l'arrivée de la saison des pluies,
Moi, qui suis professeur.

Ich fühle wenige Feuchtigkeit
der Kreide, mit der ich täglich schreibe,
weiss ich, der ich ein Lehrer bin,
die Nähe der Regenszeit.

天天用粉笔，
粉笔微潮湿，
梅雨季节近，
唯我教师知。

38. 学長とわが名小さく載りてより
　　　終日(ひねもす)電話のベル鳴り続く

Ever since my title, "president,"* began to appear in small print, the bell of my telephone keeps ringing all day.

*Elected president of Toyo University in 1985 and was in office till 1991

Depuis que ma fonction
Figure dans l'annuaire :
« Président de l'université »,
Des appels téléphoniques s'ensuivent,
Sans cesse, nuit et jour.

Seitdem mein Name als Rektor
klein in der Zeitung erscheint,
klingelt mein Telephon
den ganzen Tag.

作为一校长，
报章小载我姓名，
自此，
终日电话响不停。

39. 直立(すぐだ)てる大き杉叢影落とし
　　　河骨(かうほね)はつか揺れてゐる池

The grove of tall, straight cedars
cast its shadow
on the pond,
where yellow pond lilies sway
slightly.

Sous les ombres droites
De grands cyprès,
Subtilement se bercent
Des nuphars
Sur l'étang.

Gerade stehende hohe Zeder
werfen ihre Schatten im Taich,
wo Kawahone (eine Art von Lilie)
schaukeln im Wind nur wenig.

巨杉丛高耸，
树影落池中，
池中，
萍蓬草微动。

40. 軋(きし)む音響かせ電車曲がり行く
　　　線路に火花打ち散らしつつ

Squeaking,
the train goes
around the curve,
scattering sparks
over the railway track.

Avec des grincements aigus,
Voilà le train qui passe,
Faisant une courbe,
Laissant des étincelles
Sous ses roues.

Der Zug fährt quietschend
und schneidet eine Kurve,
indem er Funken sprühend
auf die Gleise.

电车拐弯去轰鸣，
铁轨火花四处迸。

41.　妻の書の入選知らせる文着きぬ
　　　終日氷雨の降る暮れつ方
　　　　　（ひすがら）

A notice arrives
at the nightfall
of a day when a chill rain has fallen all day,
announcing that my wife's calligraphy
has won a prize.

Une bonne nouvelle du soir
Qui annonce la selection
De l'œuvre calligraphique de ma femme
A dissipé l'ennui de toute la journée
Attristée par la pluie glacée.

Ein Brief ist gekommen, der mitteilt,
dass die Kalligraphie meiner Frau einen Preis bekommen hat,
in der Abenddämmerung des Tages,
an dem der Eisregen den ganzen Tag gefallen hat.

妻子书法作,
获选得奖项,
通知到得家,
终日雨雪夜幕下。

42.　小刻みにテーブルの珈琲揺れてをり
　　　鉄橋を電車越え行く時に

The coffee
on the table shakes
a little at a time,
as the train goes
over the railway bridge.

De légères oscillations
De ma tasse de café
Tout en harmonie
Avec les grincements du train :
Il passe sur le pont de voie ferrée.

Der Kaffee auf dem Tisch
schwankt ein wenig,
immer wenn der Zug fährt
auf den Eisenbahnbrücke.

电车过铁桥,
桌上咖啡微微摇。

43.　痛ましき事故にて知れる事多し
　　　「金属疲労」といふ語もひとつ

Many things
get known in a sad accident.
The term,
"metal fatigue,"
is one of them.

Des mots nouveaux
Parfois s'apprennent
Par quelque accident atroce.
Un exemple cruel :
« Usure métallique ».

Durch traurige Ereignisse
wissen wir viele Sachen,
eine davon ist
das Wort „Metal-Ermüdung".

事故甚惨痛,
因之长知识。
"金属疲劳"说,
亦为此类词。

44.　奔放に児童ら描く未来都市
　　　微笑(ほほゑ)ましきもありて足止(と)む

Pictures
of future cities
wildly drawn
by children are delightful,
so I stop to look at them.

Je m'arrête un instant à regarder
D'aimables tableaux des écoliers,
Représentant une cité dans l'avenir,
Réalisés avec cette liberté
Audacieuse et insouciante.

Bilder von zukünftigen Städten,
die Kinder frei und wild gemahlt haben,
sind erfreulich, so bleibe ich
stehen um sie zu schauen.

未来都市画,
儿童奔放描,
不觉止步看,
令人解颐笑。

45.　　食事にも時差にも慣れて過ぐせるや
　　　　アメリカへ典子発ちて七日目

I wonder if Noriko has got used
to American food
and the time difference.
It's seven days
since she left.

Voilà huit jours
Qu'elle est partie aux États-Unis,
Noriko. — Là-bas,
Est-elle bien habituée aux repas,
Ainsi qu'au décalage horaire ?

Es ist 7 Tage vergangen,
seitdem Noriko nach Amerika geflogen ist.
Ich sorge mir für sie, ob sie sich an die Zeitdefferenz
und das Essen schon gewohnt hat.

典子赴美国，
今乃第七日，
饮食与时差，
是否已应适？

46. 　いにしへの調べ保てる声ひびき
　　　　歌会始め今し始まる
　　　　<small>うたくわい</small>

Chanting in the voice
that retains the ancient tone,
the New Year's Poetry Party
now
gets underway.

Voilà qu'elle commence,
Première journée poétique de l'année,
Avec des récitations
Qui conservent toujours
Le parfum des jours anciens.

Das Wettdichten am Neujahr
beginnt jetzt
mit dem Klang der Stimme,
die die alten Töne bewährt.

新春第一次，
歌会刚开始。
古声古韵调，
声回四下里。

47. 柴舟(さいしう)の歌碑を説きゐるわが声を
　　かき消す程に鳴きしきる蝉

As I talk about
the tanka monument
of Saishu,*　　　　　　　*Onoe Saishu, a tanka poet (1876–1957)
the singing of cicadas is so loud
my voice is muffled.

Les chants de cigales
Si intenses
À dissiper mes voix.
Moi, essayant d'expliquer
L'histoire du monument poétique de Saishû.

Während ich das Denkmal
von Saishu erkläre,
zirpen Zikaden so laut,
daß sie meine Stimme übertöen.

解说柴舟*石碑歌，　　　　　*尾上柴舟（1876-1957），日本短
我声几被蝉鸣没。　　　　　歌诗人。

48.　母逝きて十年(ととせ)は経ちぬ年ごとに
　　　言葉少なになりゆく父か

Ten years has passed
since Mother passed away.
Father seems
to be getting more taciturn
every year.

Dix ans sont passés
Depuis la mort de ma mère.
Et chaque année,
Mon père s'enferme peu à peu
Dans son silence solitaire.

Seitdem meine Mutter starb,
ist es 10 Jahre vergangen.
Von Jahr zu Jahr
wird mein Vater wortkarg.

母亲逝世已十载,
父亲话语年年衰。

49. 初月給貰ひたる印と教へ子は
　　鈴蘭の鉢抱へつつ来る

One of my former students
brings
a pot of lilies-of-the-valley,
as a gift
bought with his first salary.

Un ancient élève vient me voir
Un pot de muguet à la main :
C'était un cadeau
Acheté pour moi
Avec son premier salaire.

Einer von meiner ehemaligen Studenten
bringt einen Topf von Maiglöckchen
als ein Geschenk,
das er von seinem ersten Gehalt gekauft hat.

说是作纪念,
头月薪水发。
一盆铃兰花,
学生抱来家,

50.　家族いまだ帰らぬ部屋に帰り来て
　　　それぞれの部屋に灯り点けゆく

While none of the family members
has come home,
I go around
into each room,
turning on the lights.

Rentré à la maison,
Où il n'y a encore
Personne de ma famille,
J'allume les pièces,
Une à une, tout seul.

Während noch niemand von meiner Familie
nach Hause gekommen ist,
gehe ich in das jede Zimmer
und mache das Licht an.

家人尚未归，
独自先到家。
打灯拉开关，
遍转各房间。

51. 「万葉」の手児奈を詠める虫麻呂の
　　　歌を説きつつ渡る継橋

We cross the Tsugihashi Bridge,
while I'm explaining the tanka
by Mushimaro,*　　　　*A poet in *Man'yoshu*
who sang of Tekona**　　**Mamano Tekona, a legendary beauty
in *Man'yoshu****　　***The 8th century anthology of Japan

Je traverse le pont Tsugihashi,
En exégète de poésies de Mushimaro
Dans le *Manyô-shû*,
Lesquelles sont des hommages
À la belle Tekona.

Wärend ich eine Mushimaro-Tanka
erkläre, die in „Manyoshu"
von Tekona sang,
gehen wir über die Tsugihashi-Brücke.

《万叶》*"手儿奈"**，　　　*《万叶集》，日本最早的歌集。
虫麻吕***曾咏，　　　　　**Tekona，真间手儿奈，也叫"真
边过木板桥，　　　　　　　间娘子"，《万叶集》中所歌美女，
边把诗歌讲。　　　　　　　追求者甚众，后因烦恼跳海自杀。
　　　　　　　　　　　　***高桥虫麻吕，万叶集歌人。

52.　コマーシャルなしに静かに鎮魂曲(レクイエム)
　　　流れゐて遂に昭和去りゆく

The serene music
of the Requiem flows
with no interruption of commercials,
while the Era of Showa*　　*The reign of Emperor Showa
goes out at last.　　　　　　(1926–1989)

Aujourd'hui
Où s'éteint l'ère de Shôwa,
Pas de publicités à la télévision.
Seul le requiem,
En toute tranquillité.

Während ein Stück von Requiem
ohne Werbefunk ruhig fließt,
geht die Showa-Zeit
endlich vorbei.

无广告插播，
唯有肃穆安魂曲，
伴随昭和去。　　　　　　　*昭和天皇（1901-1989）、昭和时
　　　　　　　　　　　　　　代（1926-1989）。

53.　この川にて投網打ちゐる人ありき
　　　杳き日に見し様さながらに

Someone is
throwing a fishing net
in this river,
just as in the days
gone by.

Sur cette rivière,
Un pêcheur
Jette ses filets sur l'eau.
Image identique à celle,
Vue dans un souvenir lointain.

Es gibt einen Menschen,
der in diesem Fluss das Netz wirft,
ebenso wie
in den alten Zeiten.

在此清川上，
有人曾撒网。
杳杳往昔事，
今仍在眼中。

54.　学会の発表明日に控へたる
　　　子の部屋の灯(あか)り漸く消ゆる

The light
of my son's room
finally goes out,
as he has prepared the paper
to be presented at the conference tomorrow.

Elle s'éteint enfin,
La lampe de la chambre de mon fils,
Qui a travaillé toute la nuit,
Préparant son exposé
Pour la réunion d'étude de demain.

Das Licht vom Zimmer meines Sohnes
geht endlich aus,
als er seine Abhandlung für einen Kongress morgen
fertig geschrieben hat.

明日有学会，
儿子要报告。
寝室照明灯，
刚刚才关掉。

55. 相撲好きの父ありせばと思ひつつ
　　　土俵ぎはなる席へと向かふ

While going
to the seat
near the sumo ring,
I wish
my father who loved sumo were alive.

Songeant avec regret
À mon feu père,
Amateur de Sumô,
Je me dirige au loge de devant,
Tout en face du *Dohyô*.

Während ich zum Platz in der Nähe
von Sumo-Ring gehe,
wünschte ich,dass mein Vater,
der das Sumo liebte, noch gelebt hätte.

想着老父亲，
喜好观相扑。
土俵*近旁席，　　　　　　　　*日本竞技运动"相扑"的竞技场地。
我今正前趋。

56.　釣り人の釣れるは鮠か木洩れ日の
　　　及ぶ河原にきらりと光る

Is it a dace
that the angler has just caught?
It glints
at the riverbed
where sun's rays fall through tree branches.

C'est bien la carpe *haya*,
Que prend le pêheur,
Poisson brillant sur la rivière ;
Laquelle est lumineuse sous le soleil
Dont les rayons traversent le feuillage.

Ist es eine Bartgrundel,
die der Angler gerade gefangen hat?
Der scheint auf im Flussbett,
wo das Sonnenlicht durch Baumkronen fällt.

树荫斑驳影，
照在河滩上。
渔人钓小鱼，
熠熠光闪亮。

57.　　腰をやや曲げて先生二階より
　　　　「やあ」と明るく下りて来給ふ

Slightly bending his back,
my mentor came
downstairs,
cheerfully saying,
"Hello!"

« Bonjour ! »
C'est mon maître qui vient
Du haut de l'escalier,
Le dos un peu courbé,
Mais avec cette gaieté toute sereine.

Mein Lehrer kam unter,
sich ein bißchen bückend
aus dem zweiten Stock,
indem er heiter sagt „Hallo".

腰板已微躬，
一声"来啦！"如洪钟，
二楼下来老先生。　　　　　*作者之恩师平野宣纪。

67

58. 葱あまた作られ鋭く匂ひをり
　　矢切の渡しへ続く道のべ

A lot of
spring onions are raised,
emitting a sharp smell
along the road
to the ferry of Yagiri.*

*A ferry crossing on the river in Matsudo, Chiba

La route qui conduit
À l'embarcadère de Yagiri,
Pleine d'odeur intense
De poireaux, qu'on cultive
Partout, dans les champs.

Sehr viel Porree werden gezüchtet.
Sie duften sehr scharf
auf dem Weg nach
der Fähre von Yagiri.

漫漫一条路，
直通矢切渡*，
两旁种大葱，
葱味冲鼻孔。

*矢切渡口，位于日本千叶县松户市。

59.　ロータリー・クラブの卓話「諾」と決め準備にかかる年末年始

As I have accepted
the Rotary Club's request
to give an after-dinner speech,
I begin preparing for it
before and after New Year's Day.

Fin de l'année studieuse,
Jour de l'an studieux,
Pour moi, qui ai accepté
La conférence
Organisée par le Rotary-club.

Ich habe angenommen, eine Tischrede
in der Rotary Club zu halten,
und fange an, um die Jahreswende
dafür vorzubereiten.

答应扶轮社，
席间去演讲。
年终与年初，
都在准备中。

60. 　打ち鳴らす鰐口(わにぐち)の音高々と
　　　　山を背に建つ寺域に響く

The gong
in the temple
sounds loudly,
resounding over the precincts
with the mountain at the back.

Des sons de *waniguchi*,
Castagnettes religieuses,
Qui retentissent, remplissant
Le sanctuaire du temple bouddhiste,
Dressé aux seins d'une montagne.

Der kupferne Schreingong
klingt laut und hallt
im Bezirk des Tempels,
der steht im Schtten des Berges.

寺院依山建,
门前铜铃铛。
清越撞铃声,
回响寺域中。

61.　書き進む原稿用紙に手の汗の
　　　　幾度か滲む夜に入りても

As I proceed with my writing
on writing paper,
perspiration from my hand
often runs on the paper
even at night.

Les feuilles de manuscrit
S'imprègnent parfois
Des sueurs de mes mains.
Continuer toujours à rédiger,
Même dans la nuit.

Ich schreibe Manuskript
noch in der Nacht.
Manchmal tropft mir der Schweiß
von meiner Hand.

一张又一张，
手汗浸湿原稿纸，
入夜亦不止。

62.　鞍馬より貴船に至る山道を
　　　遂に越えたり走り根を踏み

I have finally managed
to walk along
the mountain road
from Kurama* to Kibune,*   *Placenames in Sakyo-ku, Kyoto
stepping on tree roots exposed out of the ground.

Nous avons traversé enfin
La route de montagne,
De Kurama à Kibune,
Ayant marché parfois
Sur des racines exposées des arbres.

Ich habe endlich erreicht,
auf dem Bergpfad von Kurama
bis Kifune hinüberzugehen,
indem ich oft die Baumwurzeln trat.

出发自鞍马*,　　　　　　　　　*均为日本京都市左京区地名。
前往贵船**町。　　　　　　　**均为日本京都市左京区地名。
地面树根乱,
踏根穿山行。

63.　　対岸の小高き岩にゐる人の
　　　　釣り上げたるは鯎か光る

Is it a chub
that the angler has just hooked
on the slightly elevated rock
on the other side of the river?
It glints.

Le gain du pêcheur
Qui brille
Sur le rocher haut
De l'autre côté de la rivière,
Est-ce la carpe *ugui* ?

Ist es eine Elritze,
die der Angler auf dem höheren Fersen
am anderen Ufer jetzt gefangen hat?
Die scheint.

对岸山岩上，
渔人钓起雅罗鱼，
闪闪放亮光。

64.　鎌を持ちラベンダーの株刈りてゐる
　　　妻の横顔スナップに撮る

I take a snapshot
of the profile
of my wife
cutting a cluster of lavenders
with a sickle.

J'ai photographié,
Le profil de ma femme
Qui, une faucille à la main,
S'acharne à couper
Des pieds des lavandes.

Ich mache einen Schnappschuß
vom Profil meiner Frau,
die mit der Sichel schneidet
einen Strunk von Lavendel.

镰刀握在手,
妻子正刈薰衣草,
侧影抢拍入镜头。

65.　歌会果て夕焼け空の美しさ
　　　交々言ひてやがて別るる
　　　（こもごも）

After a tanka party
each of us praises the beauty
of the evening sky
in one's own words,
and then we break up.

Ayant terminé
La journée poétique,
Nous nous sommes séparés,
Chacun admirtant à sa façon
La beauté du couchant.

Als die Tanka-Party endete,
waren wir erstaunt über den schönen Abendhimmel,
den lobte jeder von uns mit seinem eigenen Wort
und ging bald auseinander.

歌会刚刚完，
晚霞映空多灿烂，
交谈声中各离散。

66.　デー・パックを投げ出しすぐに園児らは
　　　組んづ解れつ芝生に遊ぶ
　　　　　ほぐ

Throwing away
their daypacks,
the kindergarten kids
hustle and tussle among themselves
on the lawn.

Jetant leurs sacs à dos,
Les enfants de la maternelle
Se précipitent sur le gazon,
Pour s'amuser ensemble,
Tantôt serrés, tantôt séparés.

Gleich nach der Ankunft im Kindergarten
werfen die Kinder ihre Päcke weg
und spielen auf dem Rasen
zusammen in einer Gruppe oder auseinandertrennend.

小朋友，刚下园，
扔下背包就去玩，
时聚时分散，
草坪上面欢。

67.　蕾少し付けゐる椿に陽の及び
　　　比翼の歌碑の今し成りたり

The sun shines
on the camellia tree with a few buds.
The tanka monument, Hiyoku,*
has now been
erected.

*A tanka monument has been erected in honor of Mr. and Mrs. Nobunori Hirano. Mr. Hirano was the author's lifelong mentor

Premiers boutons de camélia
Sous le soleil ;
Voilà enfin achevé
Le monument poétique
Pour les deux âmes amoureuses.

Die Sonne scheint
auf den Kamelienbaum mit wenigen Knospen.
Das Tanka-Monument von Hiyoku
ist jetzt errichtet.

山茶花蓓蕾，
日渐增多沐春晖，
比翼歌碑今矗立。

*镌刻有作者恩师平野宣纪・纪久子夫妇所作短歌的石碑。

68.　やや小(ち)さくなり給へるか先生の
　　　背をば静かに流しゐる宵

As I gently wash
my mentor's back
at the bath,
he seems
to have shrunk a little.

N'est-il pas plus petit qu'avant ?
Me demandais-je,
Aidant mon maître
À se laver le dos,
Le soir passé à une station thermale.

Am Abend wasche ich im Bad ruhig
meinem Tanka-Lehrer den Rücken.
Er scheint ein wenig
schlank geworden sein.

老师*之背脊,　　　　　　　　　*作者之恩师平野宣纪。
渐渐在萎缩,
今宵为师静洗搓。

69.　箸袋に記されてゐる方言を
　　　話題としつつ進む夕食

While talking
about the words
from the local dialect
printed on the chopstick wrapper,
we proceed with our evening meal.

Un dîner enjoué,
Où l'on s'amuse
À discuter
Des mots dialectaux
Gravés sur l'enveloppe des baguettes.

Wir nehmen das Abendessen ein,
indem wir sprechen
von den Dialekten,
die auf der Stäbchentüte gedruckt sind.

筷囊上，
书方言，
席间成话题，
晚餐趣盎然。

70. 赴任地へと送り出さるる子の荷物
　　　妻はまた開け何加へるむ

Our son is being sent
to a place of his assignment.
My wife opens his baggage again
to put something in
on top of everything.

À cause de ma femme,
Qui ne cesse de mettre quelque chose,
Jamais ne sont finis
Les paquets pour mon fils,
Partant bientôt pour son lieu de travail.

Unser Sohn wird gesandt
auf seinen neuen Posten.
Meine Frau öffnet seine Tasche wieder
und steckt etwas hinein.

孩子调外地，
需要发行李。
包裹包好再打开，
妻子又将东西塞。

71.　　リズミカルにワープロ打つ音響きくる
　　　　深夜になりても子等の部屋より

Rhythmical sounds
of word processors
still come
out of the children's rooms
deep at night.

Des tapotements rythmiques
Sur les claviers d'ordinateur
Venant des chambres des enfants
Me font tendre l'oreille ;
Nuit profonde.

Rhythmische Klänge
des Word-Processors
kommt aus dem Zimmer meiner Kindern
noch tief in der Nacht.

儿等房间中，
优美节奏打字声，
不断传出来，
深夜亦不停。

72. 厨にて潮を吐きゐる浅蜊の音
　　物書く夜半に時をり聞こゆ

While I'm writing
at midnight,
I occasionally hear the sound
of the littleneck clams
squirting water in the kitchen.

Dans le silence de la nuit
Les palourdes laissées dans la cuisine
Laissent parfois entendre
Des sons d'eau éjectée par elles,
Signes de leur vie muette.

Als ich um Mitternacht etwas schrieb,
hörte ich ab und zu
die Stimme der kleinen Miesmuscheln,
die in der Küche Wasser spuckten.

夜半挥笔时，
偶尔可闻见，
厨房中，
蛤仔吐泥声。

73.　曇りゐて今日は樺太(サハリン)見えざりき
　　　さい果ての丘に妻と立てるに

As it was cloudy,
I couldn't see Sakhalin today,
though I stood
with my wife
on the hill at the northernmost spot.

Sous les nuages épais,
Nous n'avons pas vu l'île de Sakhaline,
Ma femme et moi,
Debout tous les deux
Sur une colline aux confins de la terre.

Da es heute bedeckt ist,
konnte ich Sachalin nicht sehen,
obwohl ich mit meiner Frau stehe
auf dem Hügel des nördlichsten Bodens.

今日是阴天，
桦太*看不见。
与妻并立望，
极北山岗巅。

*俄国地名"萨哈林"的日文说法，
　汉语为"库页岛"。

74.　おのづから足早となり登りゆく
　　　片栗の花見ゆとの声に

My pace got
quicker by itself,
as I went uphill,
hearing someone saying,
"I can see dogtooth violets in bloom!"

« Fleurs de dents-de-chien ! »
Guidé par cette voix
Venant du haut,
Je force inconsciemment mes pas
Dans la montée abrupte.

Ich ging den Hügel hoch
und beschleunigte meine Schritte,
als ich die Stimme hörte,
„Ich habe die Blumen des Hundsveilchens gefunden."

不知不觉地,
加快脚步爬。
因为山上有人喊,
"快看猪牙花!"

75. 風ありてややに揺れゐる藤の花に
　　蜂の纏（まつ）はり高くは飛ばず

Bees are hovering
around,
close to wisteria flowers
which are slightly swaying
in the breeze.

Un vent faisant balancer doucement
Les fleurs de glycine,
Les abeilles
S'entortillant autour d'elles
Ne s'envolent jamais très haut.

Bienen winden sich
um die Glyzinien herum,
die im Wind ein wenig schaukeln,
und sie fliegen nicht hoch.

紫藤花摇曳，
微风阵阵吹。
蜜蜂缠藤花，
不往高处飞。

76.　岩すべる細き流れを紫に
　　　ひととき染めて散る藤の花

Wisteria flowers
dye a thin stream
over the rocks in purple
for a short time
and then fall.

Rendant un moment tout violet
Le petit ruisseau
Qui coule sur le rocher,
Elles tombent,
Les fleurs de glycine.

Die Glyzinien-Blumen färben
den schmalen Fluß über den Felsen
kurze Zeit violett,
und dann fallen ab.

细流顺岩下，
紫藤花飞散。
花飞一瞬间，
细流为紫染。

77. 不忍の池の蓮に時をりは
　　　風渡りゆく葉裏まで見せ

Winds blow
occasionally
over the lotuses
of Shinobazu Pond,*　　　　　*It's in Ueno Park, Tokyo
revealing the reverse side of their leaves.

Uu vent frais traverse par moments
L'étang de Shinobazu
À fleur des lotus,
En renversant
Leurs feuilles vertes.

Im Shinobazu-Teich
weht der Wind ab und zu
über die Lotosblumen
und zeigt uns auch die Kehrseite ihrer Blätter.

上野不忍池*,　　　　　　　　　*日本东京上野公园西南部的水池。
荷叶铺水面。
偶尔风吹过,
掀翻叶背面。

87

78. 浴衣着て路地に集へる子供らを
　　　浮き立たせては消えゆく花火

Small sparklers
light up
the group of children wearing summer kimono
in the alley,
and go out.

Des feux d'artifice
S'éclatent et s'éteignent,
Faisant plaisir aux enfants
Réunis ici sur la rue
En kimono d'été.

Den Kindern, die im Yukata (leichten Sommerkimono)
auf der schmalen Gasse zusammentreffen,
läßt das kleine Feuerwerk das Herz aufgehen,
und geht aus.

身着夏和服*，
儿童聚小巷。
焰火烘托儿童影，
须臾又无踪。

*日语作"浴衣"，单和服，夏季、入浴后多穿着。

79.　　庭隅にローズマリーの咲き出づと
　　　　妻の言ひ出す日曜の朝

My wife says,
"Rosemaries
in the corner
of the garden started to bloom."
It's a Sunday morning.

Ma femme m'annonce
La floraison des romarins,
Tout au coin
De notre jardin ;
Dimanche matin.

Am Sonntagmorgen
sagte meine Frau,
daß in der Ecke unsres Gartens
Rosemaries zu blühen beginnen.

礼拜日早晨，
爱妻告我知：
"庭院角落上，
迷迭香花刚开放。"

80. 嫁ぎゆく前夜に娘の認（したた）めけん
　　　父母（ふぼ）あての文（ふみ）妻と読みゐる

My wife and I read the letter
our daughter wrote
to her parents
the night
before her wedding.

Ma femme et moi, tous les deux,
Lisons maintenant la lettre,
Écrite par notre fille
Hier, la veille des noces,
Avant de nous quitter.

Meine Frau und ich lesen den Brief,
den unsre Tochter an ihre Eltern
in der Nacht vor ihrer Hochzeit
geschrieben hat.

闺女出阁前，
遗信与父母[*]。
出嫁日前夜，
与妻共阅读。

[*]日本有闺女出嫁前给父母写信的习俗。

81. 帯なして届きし朝のファックスが
　　今日の予定を変へてしまへり

Faxes arrive
without a break
in the morning,
forcing me to change
my schedule for today.

Un matin
Un flux de messages
Envoyés en fac-similé
M'ont fait modifier
Les programmes d'aujourd'hui.

Die Faksimiles,
die am Morgen hintereinander
angekommen sind,
haben meine Pläne für heute geändert.

早晨接传真,
传真纸成带。
纸长须收拾,
令我今日计划改。

82.　かすかなる雪解け水の音聞こゆ
　　　木洩れ日の射す林を行くに

While I walk on
in the woods
where the sunlight comes
through tree branches,
I can hear the faint sound of snow water.

Marchant dans la forêt
Sous le feuillage
Percé partout par des rayons de soleil,
J'entends de légers bruissements
D'un ruisseau qui débâcle.

Während ich im Walde gehe,
wo die Sonne durch Bäume scheint,
höre ich ein leises Geräusch
des Schneewassers.

穿越树林中，
树荫斑驳影，
微微耳边响，
雪融水之声。

83.　研究に役立つならばと庭よぎり
　　　　錆びてかかれる錠開け給ふ

Saying, "If something I have
can be of some use for your research,"
my mentor goes across the yard
and opens the rusty lock
of his storage barn.

Traversant le jardin,
Mon maître tourne la clef rouillée,
De son magasin-bibliothèque,
Plein de documents précieux qui, dit-il,
Seront utiles pour mes recherches.

„Wenn es für Ihre Forschung nützlich sein kann",
so sagte mein Tanka-Lehrer
und geht durch den Garten hindurch,
schließt die verrostete Tür seiner Scheune auf.

穿过前庭院，
打开锈锁头。
（资料收藏者：）
"只要对您研究有帮助。"

84.　二階なる樋（とひ）に落ち葉の詰まれるや
　　　雨垂れ見つつ今日も浚（さら）へず

The eaves gutter upstairs
may have been plugged up
by fallen leaves,
but I still leave it unattended,
watching rainwater dripping.

Observant les gouttes de pluie,
Je ne peux pas encore
Curer la gouttière
Du toit du premier étage,
Pleine sans doute de feuilles mortes.

Die Dachrinne im zweiten Stock
könnte mit abgefallenen Blättern voll sein.
Aber ich kann sie heute noch nicht wegnehmen,
ich betrachte nur Regentropfen fallen.

二楼雨水管，
被落叶塞堵。
抬眼望着雨漏处，
今日亦未能通疏。

85.　新生児の部屋にすやすや眠りゐる
　　　「一希(かずき)」時をり手を頬に寄す

Kazuki* is sleeping　　　　　　　*The author's grandson born in
so sweetly　　　　　　　　　　　2000
in the nursery,
his hand occasionally touching
his cheek.

Mon petit-fils Kazuki,
Dort paisiblement
Dans la chambre de nouveaux-nés,
Pressant parfois ses mains
Sur ses joues.

Kazuki schläft sehr ruhig
in der Neugeborenenstation.
Seine Hand berührt sich
ab und zu seine Wange.

新生儿房间，
一希*睡得甜。　　　　　　　*作者之外孙。
偶尔伸小手，
够到小脸蛋。

86.　わが歌の一首に曲をつけませし
　　　楽譜の届く梅雨(つゆ)晴れの午後

It is on a clear afternoon
in the rainy season
that a sheet of music
on which one of my tanka is set to music
arrives.

C'était un après-midi ensoleillé
De la saison des pluies
Que j'ai reçu
Une feuille de musique
Destinée à un de mes tankas.

Eines schönen Nachmittags
in der Regenszeit
ist das Notenblatt angekommen,
auf dem mein Tanka vertont wird.

我有一首歌,
请人谱成曲。
乐谱送到家,
正是梅雨间晴午后时。

87.　校正の赤が右手の指に染み
　　　消えざるままに就寝となる

When I go
to bed,
fingers of my right hand
are stained with red ink
of my editorial work.

Je me couche enfin
Avec ces taches rouges
Sur la main droite,
Preuves d'un travail concentré
Pour la correction des épreuves.

Die Finger meiner rechten Hand
sind mit Rot der Korrektur gefärbt,
Während es noch so bleibt,
gehe ich ins Bett.

校对稿件时,
右手染红渍。
未能清洗净,
带红入梦乡。

88.　跡切れつつ院生謝辞を述べてをり
　　　最終ゼミを終はりし吾に

At the end
of my final seminar,
one of the graduate students
expresses his thanks,
faltering with emotions.

Mon dernier cours terminé,
Ce sont mes étudiants
Des cycles supérieurs,
Qui viennent tous me remercier, —
D'une voix entrecoupée.

Als mein letztes Seminar endete,
sprach stockend
einer meiner graduierten Studenten
ein Dankwort zu mir.

硕士博士生，
断续致谢辞。
最后研讨课，
刚刚结束之。

89.　先師あらばいかにと常に問ひ返し
　　　ためらひてのち歌稿を送る

Always wondering
how my old teacher would evaluate it,
if he were alive,
I submit my tanka,
hesitantly.

J'envoie mes morceaux de tanka
Avec toujours cette hésitation :
Mon maître,
Qu'en dirait-il
S'il était en vie ?

Ich sende das Manuskript von meinen Tankas
zögernd, nachdem ich immer wieder fragte,
wie mein alter Lehrer sie schätzen würde,
falls er noch am Leben wäre.

先师*如健在,　　　　　　　　　　*作者之恩师平野宣纪。
将会如何为?
反复自问且犹豫,
最后才将歌稿寄。

90.　夕焼けの移ろひまでも映しつつ
　　　やがて暮れゆく大きなる池

The large pond
will soon be swallowed
by nightfall,
delicately reflecting
the ever changing evening glow

Le grand lac
Qui s'obscursit peu à peu,
Reflétant le changement progressif
De la couleur du ciel,
Teint par le couchant.

Wenn die Sonne untergeht,
wird der große Teich allmählich dunkel,
indem er spiegelt
auch den Himmel im Abendrot.

广池映晚霞，
晚霞多变化。
不多时，
夜幕下。

91.　佐渡の人の暮らしの一部となりてゐむ
　　　思ひ一入(ひとしほ)能舞台見る

Intently I watch
the noh play on stage
on Sado Island,* thinking　　　*It's in Niigata Prefecture
that it must be a part
of the people's life on the island.

Je contemple
Le théâtre de Nô,
Qui me semble faire partie
De la vie
Du peuple de Sado.

Weil ich denke,
daß es ein Teil vom Leben
auf Sado-Insel geworden ist,
schaue ich das Noh-Theater eifrig an.

观看能*舞台，　　　　　　　*能剧，日本传统剧种之一。
思绪不能平。
佐渡**人生活，　　　　　　**佐渡岛，日本新潟县岛名。
能剧融其中。

92. 由布岳(ゆふだけ)を再び三たび仰ぎつつ
　　湯けむりの立つ山あひ巡る

I look up
at Mt. Yufudake*　　　　　　*It's in Oita Prefecture, Kyushu
frequently,
as I stroll along the mountain road,
where steam is rising.

En admirant par moments
La figure du mont Yufudake,
Je poursuis la route de la montagne,
Où s'élèvent partout
Des colonnes de fumée volcanique.

Ich gehe den Weg zwischen Bergen,
wo Warmwasser-Rauch steigt.
während ich zwei- oder dreimal
zum Yufudake hinaufblicke.

再三仰视由布岳*,　　　　　　*日本九州大分县火山名。
山间行,
温泉蒸汽雾腾腾。

93.　筋なして木洩れ日の射す坂道を
　　　登りて仰ぐ阿弥陀の仏

I respectfully look up
at the image of Amida Buddha,
going up the uphill road,
where streaks
of sunlight fall through tree branches.

En suivant la montée
Sous le feuillage
Percé par des rayon du soleil,
J'ai admiré par moments
Le visage d'Amida.

Ich gehe den Weg hinauf,
wo die Sonne zwischen Bäume hindurch scheint,
und blicke die Statue von Amida-Buddha
mit Respekt auf.

树荫斑驳光成行,
登坡道,
阿弥陀佛待瞻仰。

94.　これぞ彼の西行詠みたる束稲の
　　　　山ぞ桜ぞただ立ち尽くす

This is Mt. Tabashine
and these are the cherry blossoms
that Saigyo sang of,
so I just keep standing,
looking at what he saw.

Rester debout en silence,
En face du mont Tabashine
Avec ses cerisiers en fleur ;
Dans ce paysage
Admiré par Saigyô.

Das ist der Berg Tabashine und diese sind die Kirschblüte,
von denen Saigyo gedichtet hat.
So bleibe ich stehen und schaue,
was er gesehen hat.

束稻山,
樱花树,
都是那位西行曾咏物,
唯有停脚伫。

95. 満開の枝垂(しだ)れ桜の枝先が
　　水面(みなも)にはつか時をり触れる

The tips
of the weeping cherry tree in full bloom
slightly touch
the surface of the pond
from time to time.

Des brindilles pendantes
De cerisiers spachiana
En pleine floraison
Effleurant par moments
Le surface du lac.

Die Zweige der Trauerkirsche in voller Blüte
berühren ein bißchen
die Oberfläche des Wassers (des Teichs)
gelegentlich.

垂樱花盛开，
枝条垂水面。
偶尔微微动，
拂撩水面影。

96.　石畳踏みてそぞろに歩みをり
　　　小樽(をたる)運河に灯(ひ)のともる頃

I ramble
on the stone pavement
around the time
when they start putting on lights
along the Canal of Otaru.*　　*It's a city in western Hokkaido

Je me promenais
Oisivement
Sur la route pavée ;
Là-bas, s'illuminait
Le canal d'Otaru.

Mit Lust schreite ich zu Fuß
auf dem Steinpflaster,
in der Zeit, wenn man das Licht macht
auf dem Kanal von Otaru.

石板路,
漫步行,
小樽*运河初上灯。　　　*日本北海道西部地名。

97.　　満開の小彼岸桜のあはひより
　　　きらりと光る山なみの雪

Through the breaks
in rosebud cherry blossoms in full bloom
the snow
on the yonder mountain range
gleams.

Des sommets de montagnes
Couverts de neige,
Brillants, entrevus
Parmi les cerisiers subhirtella
En pleine floraison.

Zwischen den frühblühenden Kirschen
in voller Blüte hindurch
glänzt der Schnee
auf einer Bergkette.

绯樱花烂漫,
树丛间,
山雪银光闪。

98.　　カナダへの旅を是非にと話しつつ
　　　　妻遂に逝く果たせざるまま

My wife and I planned, saying
we would take a trip
to Canada by any means,
but she is gone
without realizing the plan.

En rêvant
De partir au Canada,
Elle est passée au ciel,
Toute seule,
Ma femme.

Meine Frau und ich haben geplant,
unbedingt eine Reise nach Canada zu machen,
aber meine Frau ist aus dem Leben geschieden
ohne diesen Plan zu verwirklichen.

多次告诉妻：
加拿大之旅一定去。
妻子已辞世,
诺言未能施。

99.　風花(かざはな)の舞ひ来る角度に入院の
　　　　妻のベッドを起こせしに嗚呼(ああ)

I adjusted the angle
of her bed
so that she could watch
the snow falling like cherry blossom petals,
But ah!

Je redressais parfois
Le dos du lit de ma femme,
Pour lui faire admirer
La danse de la neige — tout cela
Est maintenant un souvenir.

Ich richte das Bett meiner Frau nach draußen,
daß sie den fallenden Schnee sehen kann,
ähnlich wie die Blätter der Kirschblüte.
Aber ach!

初冬小雪花，
随风窗外舞。
摇起病床妻，
对准该角度。
（妻子未能睹，随后即逝去）呜呼哀哉！

100. 柚子二つ浮かぶを手に取り去年妻の
　　　在りし冬至を想ふ湯船に

In the bathtub
I touch two *yuzu*s* floating
with my hand, thinking
of my wife who was with us
at last year's winter solstice.

*A kind of citrous fruit. It's a Japanese custom to put some *yuzu*s in the bathtub on the winter solstice

Prenant dans les mains deux agrumes,
Qui flottent sur l'eau de bains
Du solstice d'hiver,
Je me souviens de celui de l'an dernier,
Passé avec ma femme.

In der Badewanne greife ich mir
zwei Yuzu in den Händen,
und denke von meiener Frau,
die am letzten Winteranfang noch lebte.

浴盆漂香橙*,
手拿俩沉思。
去年冬至日，
妻子尚在世。

*日本有冬至泡香橙澡的习俗。

『カナダへの旅　神作光一百首歌』に寄せて

　元東洋大学学長、神作光一さんは短歌の研究と創作の業績により2011年6月24日皇居において叙勲の栄誉を受けられました。このことは私たち東洋大学関係者と短歌関係者にとって誠にめでたく、喜ばしいことです。そしてまた、今年は神作光一さんの傘寿の年でもあり、大変めでたい年です。氏は1951年東洋大学文学部国文学科に入学されて以来、生涯を通じて平野宣紀先生に師事して短歌の研究、指導、創作に専心してこられました。神作さんの業績はいろいろありますが、なかでも一番偉大な業績は、東洋大学創立百周年記念事業として『現代学生百人一首』の募集、選歌、出版を企画、創始されたことだと私は思います。最近は毎年6万首もの応募があり若い年代の人々に短歌への関心を呼び起こし、さらには万葉時代から1300年もの歴史を持つわが国の短歌の世界に若い新風を吹き込んでいることは、実に素晴らしいことです。このようにして神作さんは我が東洋大学に『現代学生百人一首』募集、出版という輝かしい伝統を創始されたのです。この伝統は東洋大学の続く限り、受け継がれていくことでしょう。

　さて私は神作さんが約60年間に詠んでこられた短歌の中から百首を選んでいただき英、仏、独、中の四か国語に翻訳し、日本語の元歌と合わせて、五か国語による神作光一の百首歌を出版したら世界にも類のない本ができるのではないかと、ふと思いつきました。そこで中国語訳を経済学部の続三義さん、フランス語訳を朝比奈美知子さん、ドイツ語訳を堀光男さんにお願いし、ご協力を得ることができて、世界にも類のない、このようにユニークな本が出版されました。短歌には1300年もの間、日本人の心を、日本の自然の美を、歌ってきた長い伝統があります。新聞、雑誌、の歌壇を見るだけでも、短歌がいかに日本人の生活と深い関係にあるかが分かります。この百首の短歌を英訳しながら、神作さんの美しい短歌の数々に深い感動を覚えましたが、英語を知っている人々だけでなく、フランス語、ドイツ語、中国語を知っている人々にも読んでもら

えるということは、誠に喜ばしいことです。

　私は日本人と短歌がどれほど深い関係にあるかを示す一例を挙げてみたいと思います。この序文の場を借りて、鎌倉時代の説話集として著名な『古今著聞集』巻第九に所収されている「源義家衣川にて安倍貞任と連歌の事」を私なりに解釈して、英文で外国の人々にも紹介してみたいと思います。

　　伊予の国の国主源頼義が貞任、宗任たちを攻めているうちに陸奥に十二年ものあいだ滞在した。鎮守府を発って、秋田城に移動したとき、雪がはらはら降っていて、侍たちの鎧は真っ白になった。衣河の城の近くの川岸は高かったので、侍たちは盾を兜の上に重ね、筏を組んで、攻め戦っていたが、貞任側は持ちこたえきれなくなり、遂に城の後ろから逃げ始めた。
　　頼義の長男、義家は貞任を衣河に追いたてて、こう言った。「見苦しいぞ。後ろを見せて逃げるなんて。しばらく引き返せ。言いたいことがある」と。貞任が振り返ると義家が歌の下の句の形でこう言った。

　　　「ころものたてはほころびにけり」（衣の館(たて)は今や陥落してしまったぞ）

　　すると貞任は馬のくつわを緩めて馬を止め、自分の首の周りの覆いを振り向けて、歌の上の句を付けて答えてきた。

　　　「年をへし、糸のみだれのくるしさに」（長い年数の間に糸も乱れ擦り切れたのだ）

　　その時、義家は振り絞っていた矢を外して、帰っていった。このような戦いの中で、まことに優しい行動をしたものだ。

　これは極めて感動的な場面です。愛し合っている男女が、詩で掛け合

いをすることは世界中何処にでもあることですが、生きるか死ぬかの戦いの場で、敵と歌の下の句と上の句で掛け合いをするということは世界の何処の国の文学の歴史を探しても無いのではないか、と私は思います。私は長い間、『古今著聞集』のこの場面だけは広く世界に向けて英文で紹介したいと思っていました。

　神作さんの短歌の特徴は、氏の円満で優しい心根を、易しい言葉で表現していることです。恩師の平野宣紀先生、神作さんのご両親、奥様、子供、孫、教え子、に対する氏の優しい心が素直に表現されている歌は私にとって、とても感動的です。

　　背を丸め日記を綴りゐる父よ寂しくあらん母亡き五年(ごねん)

　　やや小(ち)さくなり給へるか先生の背をば静かに流しゐる宵

　　カナダへの旅を是非にと話しつつ妻遂に逝く果たせざるまま

また自然を描写する歌も美しい。

　　夕焼けの移ろひまでも映しつつやがて暮れゆく大きなる池

　　満開の枝垂(しだ)れ桜の枝先が水面(みなも)にはつか時をり触れる

　　岩すべる細き流れを紫にひととき染めて散る藤の花

　このユニークな五か国語による神作光一の百首歌を手にされている皆さん、どうぞこの本を知人、友人の方々に大いに宣伝して下さい。この本は英語、フランス語、ドイツ語、中国語を勉強している学生たちにも大いに参考になると思いますが、かつて学生時代に勉強したことのある英語、フランス語、ドイツ語、あるいは中国語の復習などにも最適だと思います。世界に類のないこの本をぜひ楽しんで読んで下さい。

　さて短歌は最近外国でもだんだん人気が出てきて、米国のユタ州あたりでは高校生対象に「タンカ・コンクール」まで行われているほどです。

この本がわが国で語学の勉強に役立つばかりでなく、外国の人々にもこの本を読んでもらい、世界に短歌を広めることの一助なれば、誠に嬉しいことです。いろいろ短歌について教えて下さった著者の神作光一さんにお礼申し上げたいと思います。そして翻訳チームに参加して下さり、素晴らしい翻訳をして下さった続三義さん、朝比奈美知子さん、堀光男さんにも心から感謝申し上げる次第です。

　2011年9月

　　　　　　　　　　　　　　　　　　　　　　　　　　　郡山　直

A Tribute from a Translator

A former president of Toyo University, Mr. Koichi Kansaku, had the honor of receiving a prestigious medal from the Emperor at the Imperial Palace on June 24, 2011 for his achievements in the field of tanka. It is really a delightful occasion for all of us concerned with Toyo University and the field of tanka. And also in the year 2011, Mr. Kansaku celebrates his eightieth birthday, which is a significant occasion for Japanese. Ever since he got enrolled in Toyo University's Japanese Literature Department in 1951, Mr. Kansaku had the late professor Tadanori Hirano for his lifelong teacher. And he has devoted himself to the studies of tanka. Tanka is a short 31-syllable poem consisting of five parts of 5-7-5-7-7 syllables. Back in 1988, Toyo University celebrated its 100th anniversary, and he initiated a significant project inviting students all over Japan to submit their choice tanka for "One Hundred Tanka by Young Students Today." It was one of the commemorative projects of the 100th anniversary of Toyo University. The annual New Year publication of "One Hundred Tanka by Young Students Today" has become a very popular event among young tanka fans of our country. Now it has more than 60,000 entries each year. It has inspired a new interest in tanka in the young people of our country and it has also breathed new life into the 1,500-year long tradition of tanka. It's publication was started by Toyo University to commemorate its 100th anniversary, when Mr. Kansaku was its president.

Mr. Kansaku taught tanka, and he composed tanka throughout his life. It just occurred to me that if we translated 100 tanka selected from all the tanka written in his nearly 60 years' career into four languages, namely, English, French, German and Chinese, we could produce a unique book, the first of its kind in the world, *100 Tanka by*

Koichi Kansaku in 5 Languages, including his original Japanese. So, I asked Professor Xu Sanyi of the Department of Economics, Professor Michiko Asahina, and Professor Emeritus Mitsuo Hori to translate the 100 tanka into each language of their specialty, Chinese, French, German, and the English translation is mine.

In the history of our country, tanka has been very popular, singing of the spirit of the Japanese people and the beauty of nature of our country for the past 1,300 years in its long tradition. Just looking at the tanka column in newspapers and magazines, we can see the close relationship between tanka and the Japanese way of life. While translating these 100 tanka, I was deeply impressed by their beauty and delicacy. And it's our pleasure to know that these tanka will be read not only by those who speak English but also by the people speaking French, German, or Chinese.

Now, taking this opportunity, I would like to cite an instance, for the readers of the world, which shows how deeply the people of Japan and tanka have been related to each other. I would like very much to expound a section from Chapter 9 of a famous collection of medieval narratives of the Kamakura period, *Kokon Chomonju*, (Records of Things Heard, Past and Present): "How Minamotono Yoshiie and Abe Sadato made a tanka by the Koromo River."

> *When Minamotono Yoriyoshi, the Lord of Iyo Province, attacked the Abe Brothers, Sadato and Muneto, he stayed in the Michinoku area for 12 years. When he left the Security Force's Headquarters and moved to Akita Castle, snow fell fluttering down, and warriors' armor was all white with snow. The riverbanks by the Robe Castle were high, so they fought, holding shields on top of their helmets, riding on the rafts they had made. Sadato's side was not able to cope with their opponents and*

began to retreat from behind the Robe Castle. Yoshiie, the oldest son of Yoriyoshi, chased after Sadato to the river, and said, "It's shameful. You run away, showing your back to us. Turn around for a while. I've got something to tell you." Then, Sadato turned back, and Yoshiie said in the form of the second half of a tanka:

> *"The warp of your robe is breaking"* (Your Robe Castle is falling down)
>
> (Note: The Japanese word for "warp" is "tate" which happens to have the same sound as an archaic word, "tate," for "castle.")

Then Sadato stopped his horse by loosening its bit, squarely turned his neck protector toward Yoshiie, and supplied him with the first half of a tanka impromptu:

> *"During the past long years, the warp got tangled and broke"*

Then, Yoshiie removed the arrow that had been fixed to the bowstring, and left the place. It was a kind action taken in such a battle scene as this.

This is a really touching scene. Men and women in love exchange their words of love in poetry all over the world, but I believe there may be no instance of two men at a critical scene of battle, each contributing the first and second part of a poem and completing it together, in the history of literature of any other country in the world. I have been thinking of introducing this passage to the readers of the world through my English translation.

Characteristics of Mr. Kansaku's tanka are clarity of imagery and simplicity of expression. His tanka expressing his mature, gentle, and delicate heart toward his lifelong master, the late professor Nobunori

Hirano, his parents, wife, children, grandchild and a former student are really impressive:

> *In a stooping position, / Father is writing his diary. / He must be lonely. / It's been five years / since Mother passed away.*
>
> *As I gently wash / my mentor's back / at the bath,*
> *he seems / to have shrunk a little.*
>
> *My wife and I planned, saying / we would take a trip / to Canada by any means, / but she is gone / without realizing the plan.*

And also his tanka depicting the delicate beauty of nature are impressive:

> *The large pond / will soon be swallowed / by nightfall,*
> *delicately reflecting / the ever changing evening glow.*
>
> *The tips / of the weeping cherry tree in full bloom / slightly touch*
> *the surface of the pond / from time to time.*
>
> *Wisteria flowers / dye a thin stream / over the rocks in purple*
> *for a short time / and then fall.*

Finally, those of you who now have a copy of this unique book, *100 Tanka by Koichi Kansaku in 5 Languages*, please tell all your friends about this book. This unique book can be enjoyed not only by students studying foreign languages but also older people who wish to brush up their skills in foreign languages.

Tanka is getting popular in other countries too. I know there was a "Tanka Contest" for high school students in the State of Utah some years ago. We translators together with the author of this book will be very happy, if this book will help spread tanka to other parts of the world. I am grateful to Mr. Kansaku for teaching me many things about tanka. And I am also grateful to Professor Xu Sanyi, Professor Michiko Asahina, and Professor Emeritus Mitsuo Hori for their excellent work for producing this book.

    September 2011

Naoshi Koriyama

著者紹介 *The Author's Profile*

神作光一　歌人・元東洋大学学長

1931年千葉県生まれ。1961年東洋大学大学院文学研究科国文学専攻博士課程修了。1985年から1991年まで東洋大学学長。現在東洋大学名誉教授。和洋学園理事。日本歌人クラブ顧問・名誉会員。「花實（かじつ）」短歌会名誉代表・選者。柴舟会常任幹事。日本詩歌句協会副会長。もやいの会会長。全日本かるた協会理事など。

現住所　〒272-0021　市川市八幡3-16-16　TEL/FAX047-324-9333

翻訳者紹介 *Profiles of Translators*

朝比奈美知子（さいしゅうかい）　東洋大学文学部教授

Ayant effectué ses études à l'université de Tokyo et à l'université de Paris XII, Michiko Asahina est actuellement professeur à l'université de Toyo. Ses travaux principaux : *Mori Michiyo*, « Expériences des Japonais à Paris », dir. H. Wada, Ed. Kashiwa, tome 20, 2011 ; *France kara mita bakumatsu ishin* (traduction des articles sur le Japon parus dans la revue *L'Illustration*), Ed. Toshindo, 2004 ; *France bunka 55 no key words* (La culture française par 55 mots clés), Ed. Minerva, 2011 ; traducton de *Vingt mille lieues sous les mers* (Verne), Ed. Iwanami, 2007 ; Contribution à la traduction des *Œuvres complètes de Nerval*, dir. T. Tamura, etc., Ed. Chikuma, 1997-2003.

堀　光男　東洋大学名誉教授

Mitsuo Hori ist im Jahre 1931 in Yamaguchi geboren. Er studierte Philosophie auf der Nagoya-Universität und Ev. Theologie auf der Universität Tübingen, wo er promovierte (Dr. theol.). Dann war er mehr als 20 Jahre lang Professor für Philosophie und Religions-wissenschaft an der Toyo-Universität tätig und emeritierte vor 10 Jahren. Werke: »Einfürung in die Ethik«, »Christentum und Europäische Gedanken-Geschichte«. Übersetzungen ins Japanisch: D. Bonhoeffer, »Versuchung«, D. Sölle, »Die Hinreise« u.a.

郡山　直　東洋大学名誉教授
Naoshi Koriyama was born on Kikai Island in the Amami chain of islands between mainland Japan and Okinawa in 1926. He studied at the University of New Mexico 1950–51 and the State University of New York at Albany 1951–54. Taught at Toyo University in Tokyo 1961–1997. Publications: *Like Underground Water: The Poetry of Mid-Twentieth Century Japan*, co-translated with Edward Lueders, (Copper Canyon Press, 1995); *Selected Poems*, (1989) and other books of poetry. Some of his poems have been reprinted in school textbooks in the USA, Canada, Australia, and South Africa.

続　三義　東洋大学経済学部教授
续三义，1954年生于中国四川省自贡市，长于山西省夏县，1973-1977就读于北京外国语学院(后为北京外国语大学)亚非语系日语专业，1977年留校任教至2007年，历任讲师、副教授、教授。前期(1977-1996)从事日语教学，后期(1996-2007)为对日汉语教学。其间，留学于东京外国语大学(1978-1980，1987-1989)、北海道大学(1986-1987)，获东京外国语大学文学修士(1989)。先后任大东文化大学客座教授(1996-1997)、台湾国立政治大学客座教授(2002-2003)、创造学园大学教授(2007-2008)。2008年至今任东洋大学教授。著作有：《对日汉语语音教程》、《日语漫步》『コミュニケーション日本語と中国語』等；译著有：《话说日本语》(日译中)、『中国語談話言語学概論』(中译日・合译)，另有日语研究、汉语研究、日汉对比语言研究论文多篇。

カナダへの旅
神作光一百首歌
〈英・仏・独・中訳付き〉

2011 年 10 月 22 日　初版発行

著　者	神　作　光　一
訳　者	郡　山　　　直
	朝比奈　美知子
	堀　　　光　男
	続　　　三　義
発行者	原　　　雅　久
発行所	株式会社 朝日出版社

〒101-0065 東京都千代田区西神田 3-3-5
電話 (03) 3263-3321
印刷：協友印刷株式会社

乱丁・落丁本はお取り替えいたします
©KANSAKU Koichi, Printed in Japan
ISBN978-4-255-00614-7 C0095